Oh, Jet!

by Jillian Powell

Illustrated by Beccy Blake

Crabtree Publishing Company

www.crabtreebooks.com

Crabtree Publishing Company
www.crabtreebooks.com
1-800-387-7650

616 Welland Ave.
St. Catharines, ON
L2M 5V6

PMB 59051, 350 Fifth Ave.
59th Floor,
New York, NY

Published by Crabtree Publishing in 2011

Series Editor: Jackie Hamley
Editor: Reagan Miller
Series Advisor: Dr. Hilary Minns, Catherine Glavina
Series Designer: Peter Scoulding
Project Coordinator: Kathy Middleton

Text © Jillian Powell 2010
Illustration © Beccy Blake 2010

Printed in Hong Kong/042011/BK20110304

First published in 2010
by Franklin Watts
(A division of Hachette
Children's Books)

The rights of the author a
illustrator of this Work ha
been asserted.

**Library and Archives Canada
Cataloguing in Publication**

Powell, Jillian
    Oh, Jet! / by Jillian Powell ; illustrated by Beccy
Blake.

(Tadpoles)
ISBN 978-0-7787-0582-6 (bound).--
ISBN 978-0-7787-0593-2 (pbk.)

    I. Blake, Beccy II. Title. III. Series: Tadpoles
(St. Catharines, Ont.)

PZ10.3.P48Oh 2011   j823'.914   C2011-900157-8

**Library of Congress
Cataloging-in-Publication Data**

Powell, Jillian.
 Oh, Jet! / by Jillian Powell ; illustrated by Bec
Blake.
    p. cm. -- (Tadpoles)
    Summary: A family is disappointed that every
they throw a toy for their dog to fetch, he brin
something else.
 ISBN 978-0-7787-0593-2 (pbk. : alk. paper) --
ISBN 978-0-7787-0582-6 (reinforced library bin
alk. paper)
[1. Dogs--Fiction.] I. Blake, Beccy, ill. II. Title.
III. Series.

PZ7.P87755Oh 2011
[E]--dc22

201005

Here is a list of the words in this story.

Common words:

a	I	said
Dad	it	that
for	Mom	we
get	not	went
go	Oh	

Other words:

| boy | Jet | took |
| good | swim | walk |

We took Jet

for a walk.

"Go get it!" Mom sai

4

"Not that!" Mom said.

"Oh, Jet!" I said.

7

"Go get it!" Dad sai

"Not that!" Dad said.
"Oh, Jet!" I said.

12

et went for a swim.

"Go get it!" Dad said.

15

16

"Good boy!"
Dad said.

"Oh, Jet!" we said.

21

Puzzle Time

a

b

 Can you find these
pictures in the story

c

d

Which pages are
the pictures from?

Turn over for the answers!

Answers

The pictures come from these pages:

a. pages 16 and 17
b. pages 4 and 5
c. pages 10 and 11
d. pages 20 and 21

Notes for adults

Tadpoles are structured to provide support for early readers. The stories also be used by adults for sharing with young children.

Starting to read alone can be daunting. **Tadpoles** help by listing the word the book for a preview before reading. **Tadpoles** also provide strong visu support and repeat words and phrases. These books will both develop confidence and encourage reading and rereading for pleasure.

If you are reading this book with a child, here are a few suggestions:

1. Make reading fun! Choose a time to read when you and the child are re and have time to share the story.

2. Look at the picture on the front cover and read the blurb on the back co What might the story be about? Why might the child like it?

3. Look at the list of words on page two. Can the child identify most of the words?

4. Encourage the child to retell the story using the jumbled picture puzzle pages 22-23.

5. Discuss the story and see if the child can relate it to his or her own experiences, or perhaps compare it to another story he or she knows.

6. Give praise! Children learn best in a positive environment.

If you enjoyed this book, why not try another **TADPOLES** story?
Please see the back cover for more **TADPOLES** titles.
Visit **www.crabtreebooks.com** for other **Crabtree** books..